The Sleepover Club

*Have you been
invited to all these
sleepovers?*

The Sleepover Club at Frankie's
The Sleepover Club at Lyndsey's
The Sleepover Club at Felicity's
The Sleepover Club at Rosie's
The Sleepover Club at Kenny's
Starring the Sleepover Club
The Sleepover Girls go Spice
The 24 Hour Sleepover Club
The Sleepover Club Sleeps Out
Happy Birthday, Sleepover Club
Sleepover Girls on Horseback
Sleepover in Spain
Sleepover on Friday 13th
Sleepover Girls at Camp

Sleepover Girls
go Detective

by Louis Catt

Collins

An Imprint of HarperCollins*Publishers*

The Sleepover Club ® is a
registered trademark of HarperCollins*Publishers* Ltd

First published in Great Britain by Collins in 1999
Collins is an imprint of HarperCollins*Publishers* Ltd
77-85 Fulham Palace Road, Hammersmith,
London, W6 8JB

1 3 5 7 9 8 6 4 2

Text copyright © Louis Catt 1999

Original series characters, plotlines
and settings © Rose Impey 1997

ISBN 0 00675393-0

Printed and bound in Great Britain by
Caledonian International Book Manufacturing Ltd,
Glasgow G64

Sleepover Kit List

1. Sleeping bag
2. Pillow
3. Pyjamas or a nightdress
4. Slippers
5. Toothbrush, toothpaste, soap etc
6. Towel
7. Teddy
8. A creepy story
9. Food for a midnight feast:
   chocolate, crisps, sweets, biscuits.
   In fact anything you like to eat.
10. Torch
11. Hairbrush
12. Hair things like a bobble or hairband,
    if you need them
13. Clean knickers and socks
14. Change of clothes for the next day
15. Sleepover diary and membership card

CHAPTER ONE

Hello – and I'm very pleased to see you. I'd like to welcome you to the Sleepover Club.

There! Isn't that better than Frankie or Kenny? They just jump straight into the story, and my mum says you should *always* be polite. The others tease me because I don't really like rushing about the way they do – but I think *someone* has to be sensible, don't you? My mum says that sometimes the others get too wild, and she doesn't like me to be like that. Sometimes it *is* funny, though. I mean, when we were pretending to be yowling cats outside Mrs Brierley's house and she threw a bucket of water over Frankie and Rosie... but I shouldn't be telling you that now. (Don't worry – I won't forget to tell you all the details when I get to that bit in the story!)

Perhaps I should have started by saying "How do you do?" Or maybe that's too much? Anyway, I'm Felicity Diana Sidebotham, and I'm ten. I'm the oldest in the Sleepover Club. My birthday is September 16th; I used to mind, because it meant I was always the oldest in the class, but I don't mind so much now. I rather like it.

If you want to know what I look like I've got really truly blonde hair, and I'm very slim. My mum says I've got a very good figure, and she ought to know. She's a beautician. It's nice having a mum who knows about hair and beauty things; my mum is always careful about what she eats, and I am too. I don't want to get fat. *Gross*!

I live with my mum and my stepdad, Andy, and I've got a little brother called Callum. Sometimes he's OK, but sometimes I wish he was a girl. If he was a girl I could talk to him about clothes and things. My real dad got married to someone else and they've got a lovely little baby girl, but she's much too young to talk to. She's very pretty, though. My mum says I'm pretty too, but sometimes I'm not sure. It's difficult to tell when you look at your own face in the mirror. When Callum wants to wind me up he says my nose is like a great big squashed tomato, but I don't think it is. Not really. It's just Callum being a boy.

Don't you think girls are much nicer than boys? I mostly do – except for Ryan Scott. He's in our class at school. He's a brilliant footballer, and he's very interesting to talk to. Well, that's what I think – although Frankie and Kenny and Lyndz and Rosie just laugh when I say so. My mum says they're jealous because he likes me better than them, but I don't think they really care.

Do you know the other members of the Sleepover Club? There's Frankie and Kenny – they're best friends. Actually, sometimes – just between you and me – I feel a tiny bit left out when we're at school. And sometimes I even feel like that when we're having a sleepover. Frankie and Kenny get on really well together, and they love playing tricks, and I don't. Once they put pretend blood all over Kenny's garden path, and I thought it was real... I nearly fainted! My knees went completely wobbly and I felt swimmy in my head and Rosie said afterwards that my face went green. Kenny had to get me hot sugary tea, and wrap me up in a duvet. Did you know that's what you do if someone has a bad shock? Kenny wants to be a doctor when she grows up, so she's good at knowing things like that. Her dad's a doctor.

Oh! I'm not being very organised. I hope you're not muddled! I'll go back to the beginning and tell you about the others properly.

Frankie first. She doesn't have any brothers or sisters. She's got a pet dog called Pepsi, though. I like Pepsi because she isn't the sort of dog who jumps up and puts her muddy paws all over you. A long time ago Frankie had

10

a cat called Muffin who got run over, and if you think it's odd that I'm telling you about a dead cat, it isn't. If Frankie hadn't still been missing Muffin she wouldn't have— *whoops*! I keep forgetting that this is the introduction, and I mustn't tell you too much of the story yet. Perhaps you could just remember about Muffin, though.

Then there's Kenny. Like I told you, she wants to be a doctor. She's got two sisters, and she has to share her bedroom with her sister Molly. I'm really glad I don't have to share with anyone. Molly is *horrible* – we call her Molly the Monster. She's always complaining about Kenny – although I do think Kenny is a bit untidy. If you look under her bed you'll see it's *stuffed* with dirty clothes. There's even a big bag of rat food – UGH!!! Luckily the rat is in the garage. I don't think I'd ever be able to sleep over at Kenny's house if the rat was in her room like she wants it to be. I'd have terrible dreams about scaly tails and horrible sharp teeth all night long.

I haven't told you about Lyndz and Rosie

yet. Rosie is like me; she doesn't live with her dad. She's got a big sister, Tiffany, and an older brother called Adam who uses a wheelchair. Her house is a bit like Lyndz's house; it's very messy and a lot of the walls need painting. Rosie says her dad keeps promising he'll come back and sort it out, but he doesn't. I don't think I'd like to have Rosie's room at all. My bedroom has ever such pretty wallpaper, and my mum let me choose my curtains and my rug.

Who haven't I told you about yet? Oh yes – Lyndz. She's got two brothers who are older than her, and two younger ones. She lives in a big untidy house with things all over it, and her dad is always doing stuff to it. I think they should ask my stepdad, Andy, to do it properly (he's a very neat plasterer) but they don't. It's odd, but they seem to like it just the way it is… and I suppose it is sort of comfortable. You never have to worry about spilling things or keeping the cushions all nice and puffed up like we do in my house. Lyndz has a dog, but I don't like him as much as

Frankie's. He barks all the time, and he rushes about. Sometimes he jumps on your lap, and his paws are all wet and muddy and disgusting. There are three cats too... Toffee, Fudge and Truffle. It was because of Truffle that we turned into detectives... because one day Truffle went missing!

CHAPTER TWO

When Truffle disappeared, Lyndz was really upset. She was late arriving at school, and her eyes were red. Mrs Weaver – our teacher – told her that cats often wander off on their own for a bit, but Lyndz said Truffle *always* comes in at six o'clock for her kitty crunchies.

"When did you last see her?" Frankie asked.

"Yesterday morning," Lyndz said, and she sniffed loudly. "She was licking the butter and I shouted at her. Maybe she's run away because I was so horrible."

"*Yeah!*" The M&Ms grinned at each other. "Cruel – that's what you are! *Poor* little pussy.

She's run away to live with people who will be kind to her!"

Have I told you about the M&Ms? Their real names are Emma Hughes and Emily Berryman, and they hate us and we hate them. They're always trying to get one up on us – sometimes they are just so mean.

This time it looked as if they'd been really successful. Lyndz turned her back on them, but I could see her shoulders were shaking. She was blowing her nose really hard. I glared at the M&Ms, and so did Kenny.

"If you think it's funny making jokes about someone's lost cat you're even grosser than we thought you were!" Kenny said.

The M&Ms tried not to grin, but they couldn't quite stop. Lyndz went on worrying. "It was so cold last night, too," she wailed. "Truffle *never* stays out all night. She sleeps on the end of my bed, and keeps my toes warm."

Frankie put her arm round Lyndz's shoulders just as one of the M&Ms whispered to the other, and they fell about shrieking with laughter.

"What's so funny?" Frankie asked them.

They didn't answer, but went on giggling.

Frankie went right up to them, and Kenny went with her.

"Tell us what the joke is!" Frankie said, and she sounded terribly fierce.

Emma stopped laughing. "We were only fooling around," she said. "I'm sorry if you're worried."

They didn't look sorry at all. "Cats are always going off," Emily said. "Our cat goes out every night." She began to snigger again. "We were wondering if your mum thought your cat was a hot water bottle and hung it up in a cupboard!" And then they both laughed all over again.

I wanted to tell Mrs Weaver, but Lyndz said it wasn't worth it. She said we'd always known the M&Ms were totally pathetic, and the way they were going on just proved it.

"Take no notice of them," Rosie said. "If we do it'll only make them worse."

I think Rosie was right. She knows quite a lot about how to treat people; I think it might be because sometimes stupid people call her brother names.

The bell went then, and we had to go back into lessons. Mrs Weaver was very nice to Lyndz, which was just as well as Lyndz got all her spellings wrong.

Halfway through the afternoon I saw Frankie pass Lyndz a note.

Lyndz read it (Mrs Weaver was writing something on the board) and then she passed it on to me. It said:

HEY! I'VE HAD AN IDEA! IF TRUFFLE ISN'T AT HOME TONIGHT SOMEONE MUST HAVE STOLEN HER... SO WE'LL BE THE SLEEPOVER DETECTIVES AND TRACK HER DOWN!!!!

I looked at Lyndz, and she was sitting up much straighter and smiling at Frankie. I passed the note on to Rosie, and she read it too. Then Kenny got it, and she said "YES!" so loudly that Mrs Weaver turned round.

"Am I missing something?" she asked.

We all tried to look as if we had been

working extra specially hard. Of course the M&Ms had to blurt.

"They were passing notes, Mrs Weaver," Emma said, and she gave us a huge fat horrible smile.

"That's right, Mrs Weaver," Emily said. "We both saw them."

Now, Mrs Weaver usually hates us passing notes more than anything else. She says it's underhand, and that if we have something to say we should stand up and say it. She says it is really rude, and means we don't respect her at all. This time, though, she gave Emma and Emily a funny look.

"Thank you," she said. "If ever I want a report on the private activities in my class I'll remember to ask you two. In the meantime, however, I suggest you all get on with what you're doing."

That squashed the M&Ms! We could hardly believe our luck. We put our heads down and worked really hard until the end of the lesson – which was also going-home time.

When we'd cleared up and put our chairs

on the tables, Frankie went straight up to Mrs Weaver. She was holding the note in her hand. She walked right past the M&Ms, and I saw them staring.

"I'm sorry, Mrs Weaver," Frankie said, "but I did pass Lyndz a note. It wasn't a bad one, though. You can read it – I just wanted to cheer her up."

Mrs Weaver smiled at Frankie, and dropped the note in the wastepaper basket.

"I had a feeling it was something like that," she said. "Don't do it again, though." And she went on clearing up, still smiling.

The M&Ms looked as sick as parrots!!!

When we got outside the school gate Frankie let out a loud "WHOOPEE!!!" and we all joined in. Then Kenny said we should give three cheers for Mrs Weaver, so we did that too. (I think it was a little bit louder than it might have been because the M&Ms were walking past exactly at that moment!)

Then Frankie grabbed Lyndz's arm. "Can you ring us if Truffle's still missing?" she asked her. "And if she is we'll make a Grand Plan!"

"Sleepover Detectives!" Rosie said, and she whacked Lyndz on the back in an encouraging sort of way.

Kenny giggled. "We can't catnap if we're looking for a catnapper," she said.

"But we'll catch the catnapper who's napping with the cat!" Frankie said.

"We can pore over her paw prints and follow the trail to her tail!" Rosie chipped in.

We all laughed then, even Lyndz.

"I'll ring as soon as I get home," she promised.

I'd been thinking while the others were telling jokes. (I'm not very good at being funny.) I wasn't sure what we could do if we were detectives; I was worrying that we didn't have things like magnifying glasses and cameras, and all the other things detectives need.

"What exactly will we do?" I asked. "I mean, if she hasn't come home? Where will we look first?"

Frankie stopped grinning and rubbed her nose. "Maybe we should check out the pet shop. Maybe someone might have found her and thought she was a stray."

"Wouldn't they take her to a cats' home?" Kenny said. "Or the RSPCA?"

"She's got our phone number on her collar," Lyndz said, and she began to look unhappy again. "If someone had found her they'd have rung up."

"Could she have lost her collar?" I asked. Rosie nodded.

"Our cat wriggles out of his quite often. It's because you mustn't put their collars on too tight."

"She might have lost it," Lyndz said. "Actually, it was a bit loose, and it had one of those elasticky bits on it."

"Well then!" Kenny waved her arms in the air. "Probably she got stuck in a tree or something yesterday, and she wriggled out of her collar this morning—"

"And she's sitting on your bed at home now this minute!" Rosie yelled.

Lyndz smiled at us. "Thanks," she said. "I do feel better now."

"Will you ring us anyway, even if she's back?" I asked.

"Of course I will." Lyndz picked up her bag. "I'll zoom back and see right this minute." She dashed off, and we all went home too.

CHAPTER THREE

I'd only been at home about ten minutes when the phone rang. It wasn't Lyndz – it was Frankie. She said Lyndz's mum had told Lyndz she could only ring two of us and we were to pass the message on. Anyway, Frankie said Truffle was still missing, and we were all going to go to the pet shop after school tomorrow.

"We could come back to my house afterwards to make a plan if Truffle's not there," I said.

"Actually," Frankie said, "everyone's coming to my house. I've already arranged it. Oh, and

Lyndz's mum says she can have a sleepover at her house next Friday to cheer her up… or if Truffle's back it can be a celebration! OK?"

"Yes," I said. "All right."

"See you tomorrow, then," Frankie said, and she rang off.

I put the phone down too, Sometimes Frankie can be very bossy. We hardly ever meet up after school at my house, and my house is much the nicest. My mum really likes it when everyone come round too, and she makes us special cakes and buys lots of different kinds of biscuits.

We had to wait for my brother Callum before we could go to the pet shop the next day. He walks home with me, and my mum says he's not old enough to come home on his own. His class was late coming out; because they're younger they seem to take ages and ages getting their coats on.

While we were waiting, Lyndz told us she'd been doing some detective work on her own.

"The last person who saw Truffle was Mum," she said. "Truffle was bouncing out of the cat flap, and she looked just like she always does. And we've checked all the cupboards and sheds and drawers, because a friend of Mum's said her cat got into her airing cupboard and was shut in for six days while they were away on holiday!"

"Was the cat OK?" Rosie asked.

Lyndz nodded. "Yes. It was very thin, but it was completely fine as soon as it had had something to eat!"

Kenny was looking thoughtful. "What did the airing cupboard look like?"

I knew exactly what she was going to ask about. Kenny always wants to know about disgusting things. Luckily just at that moment Callum came round the corner, so I jumped up.

"Look!" I said. "There's Callum! Let's go!"

Callum was a bit grumpy about having to go to the pet shop, but he cheered up when Lyndz told him about Truffle. She's got younger brothers too, so she knows how to talk to him.

"I'll look out for her," he said. "I'm very good at seeing things."

25

We all squeezed into the pet shop together. It isn't very big, so we more or less filled it up. There were cages all over the walls, and all round the floor too. I didn't mind the ones with birds peeping and cheeping, but I didn't look at the ones with horrible squirmy little rats and mice in.

Mr Garez didn't look very pleased to see us, which is unfair because the customer is always right. Besides, Lyndz buys loads of rat food from his shop, and Frankie's mum buys dog food there.

"I hope you've come for a reason," he said. "I'm fed up with kids coming in just to look at the kittens. This is a shop, not a zoo."

"Kittens!" Kenny said. "Oh, Mr Garez – where are they?"

Mr Garez sighed very loudly and pointed at a big cage in the corner – and there they were. Three tabby kittens, and a tiny fluffy black one that was chasing its tail round and round and round.

"OH!" Frankie nearly fell over her feet in her rush to look closer. "LOOK! He's *exactly* like Muffin!"

"Who's Muffin?" Rosie asked her.

"He was my cat who died," Frankie said. "He was *lovely*, and I still miss him. He was black all over with a tiny white spot under his chin – oh, Mr Garez, *please* can I hold him? Just for a minute?"

Mr Garez sighed again, even louder than before, but he came over to the cage. "He's a little terror, that one," he said as he fished the black kitten out and plopped it into Frankie's hands. "He's forever getting out. I'll be glad when someone takes him."

Frankie was gazing at the kitten, and her eyes were shining. "I'll take him!" she said. "My mum and dad won't mind – we've still got Muffin's food bowl in the cupboard! How much is he?" And she started pulling her purse out of her pocket with one hand while she cuddled the kitten with the other.

Kenny, Rosie, Lyndz and I stared at her.

"Are you sure your mum and dad won't mind?" Rosie said. "I mean, shouldn't you at least go home and ask?"

Frankie shook her head. "I *know* they'll be pleased," she said. "Mum knows how much I miss Muffin, and Pepsi's getting much older now – she'll be thrilled to have another animal to play with!"

"Meow," said the kitten. It was funny! It was just as if he had understood every word Frankie was saying.

Frankie looked desperate. "I *have* to have him!" she said. "LOOK! You can see he knows he belongs with me!"

"Five pounds," said Mr Garez. "The owner said five pounds to a good home."

Frankie tucked the kitten inside her jacket, and opened her purse. "Can anyone lend me a pound?" she asked. "I've only got four – no, four pounds twenty."

We scrabbled about in our pockets. Rosie had ten pence, and Lyndz had fifty. I didn't have any money at all, and neither did Kenny.

Mr Garez watched while we piled up the money on the counter.

"H'm," he said. "Four pounds eighty. Maybe I do a discount for bad kittens," and he actually smiled as he scooped the money up and put it in the till.

"Thank you!" Frankie said. "He'll be the happiest kitten EVER!"

We stroked the little tabby kittens while Mr Garez stumped off into the back of the shop. I wished I could have had one, but Mum says pets aren't hygienic. Also she says they give Callum asthma, although he never gets asthma when he plays with animals at other people's houses.

Mr Garez came back with a piece of paper and a big cardboard box with holes in it.

"Here you are," he said, and he gave Frankie the paper. "He's had all his injections. Feed him four small meals a day, and make sure he has water where he can reach it. Now, pop him in the carrying box to take him home." Mr Garez smiled again. "And don't bring him back! I'm too old to chase him all round the shop five times a day!"

We were just about to walk out when I remembered why we'd come to the shop in the first place.

"Please," I said, "has anyone brought in a lost cat?"

Lyndz jumped round. "Wow, Fliss!" she said. "Well done! How *could* I have forgotten poor old Truffle?"

But Mr Garez said that he hadn't heard anyone talking about a lost cat, and they certainly hadn't brought one in.

"If we write a notice will you put it up in the window?" I asked.

"Of course." Mr Garez seemed really happy now. "Bring it in, and I'll be pleased to do that."

Once we were outside Lyndz gave me a hug. "That's a mega-brilliant idea about the notice," she said. "We'll write a whole lot out at Frankie's house, and ask all the other shops as well. Do you think we could use your dad's computer, Frankie?"

"H'm?" Frankie wasn't listening. She was holding the big cardboard box very very carefully, and was trying to squint in through one of the holes.

"Can we use your computer?" Lyndz asked.

"I expect so," Frankie said. "Dad'll probably

be there when we get back. He and Mum were going out somewhere together this afternoon – don't ask me where. They wouldn't tell me – it seems to be some sort of secret."

"Ooh!" Kenny said. "Tell us more!"

Frankie grinned. "It's something to do with holidays, because when I asked Mum where we were going next summer she looked at Dad, and then he winked at her, and then they both said next summer would be a real surprise... but I'd have to wait for a bit to find out."

"Oh." Kenny sounded disappointed. "Grown ups are so boring."

Rosie suddenly clutched my arm. "FLISS!" she said. "Where's Callum?"

CHAPTER FOUR

We pounded back into the pet shop. My heart was fluttering, but I needn't have worried. Callum was sitting on the counter chatting to Mr Garez – and he was holding a rat!

EEEEEEEEEEEEEEEEEKKKK!!!!!

I didn't mean to scream. It was the surprise – and it was such a BIG rat! It was a fast runner, too. When I screamed the rat and Callum jumped – but the rat jumped higher. Callum and Mr Garez both grabbed at it, and they both missed – and the rat scuttled off at a hundred miles an hour.

"I can see it!" Callum yelled, and he flung

himself on to the floor. He didn't mean to knock over the bag of rabbit food, but it tottered... and then crashed to the floor almost on top of him. Crunchy bits and grassy bits spread absolutely everywhere.

"STOP!!!!!" yelled Mr Garez. "STOP – before I have no shop left!"

Callum froze... and so did the rest of us. I'm sure Frankie and Kenny were completely cracking up laughing, but they hid behind the kitten's cardboard box so Mr Garez couldn't see.

"Now, OUT!" said Mr Garez, and Frankie, Kenny and Rosie zoomed out through the door. Lyndz grabbed Callum's hand, and followed them, and I was going to go too, but I didn't. I really did feel bad about the mess – and after all, Callum is my brother.

I took a deep breath, and I swallowed hard.

"Mr Garez," I said, "I'm *very* sorry."

Mr Garez glared at me. "I should hope so!" he said. "*Look* at all this mess! I should tell your mother!"

"I'll help you sweep it up," I said, and then I

nearly flipped. The rat had come sneaking back out and was nibbling at the rabbit food – and *another* rat had come out too! A HUGE black rat!

I would have screamed again, but I couldn't. My tongue was stuck in my mouth. I couldn't do anything except stare.

Mr Garez swooped down – and picked up both rats – first the brown one, and then the huge black one. Would you believe that he seemed really really pleased to see the black one? He even gave it a little kiss!!! YUCKKKK.

"Aha!" said Mr Garez. "So *there* you are, my pretty friend!"

GROSS!!! Mr Garez had a rat in each hand, and their bristly, scaly tails were twisting round his fingers! I wanted to shut my eyes, but I couldn't.

The rats were soon safely back in their cage, and Mr Garez shut the door with a click. "So – you frighten my rat, young lady, and you spill my rabbit food – but you find me my prize rat while you do it! Maybe we should say that we are quits. And maybe you should go quickly before I change my mind!"

I nodded. I still couldn't say anything. I just headed for the door.

"If your little brother wants a rat," Mr Garez called after me, "I can get him one! Very cheap, too!"

"NO – er – thank you," I called back, and I rushed after the others.

Callum talked about rats all the way back to Frankie's house. The trouble was he'd heard Mr Garez, and he asked me over and over how much 'very cheap' was. I kept telling him to be quiet, but then Kenny told him how great rats are. It's no good, though. My mum would rather have an alien living in the house than a rat. Actually, I think I'd rather have an alien too.

Frankie was right. When we got to her house both her parents were at home. They were sitting have a cup of tea in the kitchen, and they looked – I don't know – pleased with themselves. Anyway, they seemed pleased to see us too, even Callum. Frankie's mum opened a new box of biscuits and her dad put on the kettle.

"So – what ghoulish surprise are you keeping in the box, Frankie?" her dad said as we marched in. "Some horrible sleepover special?"

Frankie went very pink. "Oh, *Dad*!" she said. "It's the most heavenly thing that's happened to me since Muffin died! LOOK!" And she opened the cardboard box.

I don't know what that kitten had been doing in the box. He'd been dead quiet all the way home; not a squeak or a meow. He must have been planning his arrival at Frankie's house. He came out of that box like a furry black streak, and he went straight up the curtains and meowed so loudly you could have heard him six doors down.

Frankie's mum jumped up, and Frankie's dad dropped the milk jug. Callum shouted, and Frankie rushed after the kitten calling, "Muffin! Muff, muff, muff! Don't be frightened!" The kitten jumped; he jumped off the top of the curtains, and he landed on the draining board. It was full of glasses and cups, and he kind of slid along the shiny surface with them… only *they* fell on the floor and he didn't.

"Whoops!" said Rosie, and she ran to head him off, but he did a quick turn and leapt on to the table. Kenny grabbed at him, but he was much too quick. He shot back up the curtains, climbed to the top and hid behind the curtain rail.

"FRANKIE!" said her mum. "*Whatever* is that?"

"He's just scared," Frankie said. "He'll come down in a minute – oh, don't you think he's the most *blissful* kitten in the whole wide world?"

Frankie's dad finished wiping the milk off the floor, and stood up with the wet drippy cloth in his hand.

"I think we should let that animal calm down," he said. "If everyone keeps on chasing it we'll never catch it."

"He'll come down soon," Frankie said. "He's just getting to know us all. Mum, where did we put Muffin's old bowl?"

Frankie's mum looked at her in that way parents do when something is Very Bad News.

"Oh, Frankie!" she said. "Whatever were you thinking of? We *can't* have a kitten – I'm sorry, but there's no way it's possible. I don't know where you got that one from but he'll have to go back."

I felt so sorry for Frankie. I know she's bossy and sometimes she gets too big for her boots and tries to tell us what to do, but anybody would have been sorry for her then. She looked at her dad, and he shook his head.

"Sorry, poppet," he said. "No can do. Wait until he's come down off his mountaineering expedition, and take him home."

"I can't," Frankie said, and there was a wobble in her voice. "Mr Garez said I couldn't. He said he didn't want him back. And," – she looked up at the clock – "his shop is shut now."

"The kitten could come to my house for the night," Lyndz said. "If that would help, that is."

Frankie's mum smiled. "That's very kind of you, Lyndsey – but we can probably manage for tonight." She patted Frankie's hand. "Just don't get too fond of him. I'm not going to change my mind."

38

Frankie nodded. She didn't say anything, and I think it was because she would have cried if she'd had to open her mouth.

"What were you doing in the pet shop anyway?" asked Frankie's dad. Lyndz had seen Frankie's face too, and she bounced up.

"We were asking about my cat, Truffle," she said. "She's disappeared, and we thought someone might have found her and taken her to the pet shop." She sighed. "But they hadn't."

"There were LOTS of rats!" Callum piped up. "One of them had got out, and Fliss found it! And I want a rat of my own."

"Goodness me," Frankie's dad said. "Missing cats, found rats, mad kittens – whatever next?"

Just then the kitten came down from the curtain. He skipped across the floor, and began to lick the tiles where the milk had spilt.

"Can I give him some water with a little milk in it?" Frankie asked, and her mum nodded.

"Take him up into your room as soon as he's drunk it. And you'd better take his box with you – oh, and put some newspapers in

Muffin's old litter box. Is he house trained?"

"I don't know," Frankie said, and she went very slowly to fetch the milk.

CHAPTER FIVE

You should have seen us sitting in Frankie's bedroom! GLOOM. MEGA GLOOM. And then MEGA MEGA GLOOM.

That's not like us. If you know anything at all about the Sleepover Club you'll know we're usually falling about or cracking up about something. But there we were – and even with scrummy chocolate biscuits in front of us we all had faces as long as fiddles.

Frankie was sitting with the kitten on her lap. He was looking as if he'd never climbed a curtain in his life, and making this cute little purring noise.

Lyndz was staring out of the window. Rosie was slumped against the wall. Kenny was frowning at her feet. I was watching the kitten. I couldn't believe that Frankie couldn't keep him. I mean, my mum has *always* said no pets, but Frankie's got a dog, and a cat is much easier to keep. You don't have to take them for walks, and they don't need playing with the same way a dog does.

Thinking about cats made me remember Truffle, and I sat up.

"I'll have to take Callum home soon," I said. (I'd left him downstairs watching the Simpsons. He just LOVES the Simpsons.) "Are we going to make those notices about Truffle?"

No one answered at first, and then Lyndz suddenly leant forward. She pointed out of the window.

"Hey! Fliss – can you see a cat over there on the wall?"

I hurried to look, but I couldn't see any cat. Frankie got up and carried the kitten to the window so they could both look out.

"Oh – that's one of Mrs Brierley's cats," she

said. "She's got *dozens* of cats – I think she collects them or something."

"LYNDZ!!!" Kenny rushed to the window too. "If she collects cats maybe she's collected Truffle! Maybe she goes round the streets with a cat bag—"

Rosie nodded. "And she calls, 'Kitty, kitty'! And she has smelly fish heads in her bag—"

"And when they come running she snatches them up and hurries home to add them to her collection!" Lyndz said. Then she looked really worried. "Do you think she might have taken Truffle?"

"Only one way to find out," Frankie said. "We'll go and see!"

"We can't!" I said. "We can't march in and say, 'We've come to check out your cats'!"

"We could – we could offer to do odd jobs for her!" Frankie said. "My mum's always saying she's a poor old thing who could do with some help! We could say we're—"

"Boy scouts!" said Kenny. "My dad says boy scouts used to come round to his house once a year and say 'Bob a job!' And whatever you asked them to do they did, and it only cost a bob. Dad says that's about five pence!"

"We *can't* be boy scouts," I said, and for some reason all the others cackled with laughter.

"It's good idea, though," Rosie said. "We could do – er—"

"Weeding!" Frankie said. "Her garden's full of weeds! And that would give us a brilliant excuse for spying on Mrs B and checking out the cats!"

Rosie moaned loudly. "I HATE weeding."

"Me too," said Kenny. "But detectives have to be ready to take on any disguise! Tomorrow we'll be the Sleepover spies – undercover in the garden!"

"I'd rather be a cabbage," Rosie said.

"You already are!" said Frankie, so Rosie threw a pillow at her. The kitten took off and Kenny dived for him and missed. Frankie threw the pillow back at Rosie, but Rosie ducked – and it landed FLOP!!! on the plate of chocolate biscuits.

*　　*　　*

44

When we had caught the kitten again and picked some of the biscuit crumbs off the carpet we went back to the plan.

"I'll ask Mum," Frankie said. "She's bound to say yes to us being helpful. Then we can knock on Mrs Brierley's door after school. She's always there in the afternoons."

Rosie nodded. "I expect she goes cat catching at night."

"Out in the dark, with the cats' eyes shining!" Kenny said.

"We won't wait until it's dark though, will we?" I asked.

"Who knows where the hunt will take us!" Frankie said, and she flung out her arms in an actorish way.

"We may have to go creeping through the bushes, and hunting in dark corners!" Kenny hissed.

"Hiding behind ancient creaking doors, while the slow, dragging footsteps pass by..." whispered Frankie.

"But it doesn't get dark until quite late," I said. "I can't stay out until then."

"Nor can we," Rosie said. "But we can imagine it—"

Lyndz sighed. "Wouldn't it be brilliant if Truffle really was there?"

"Tomorrow will reveal all!" said Frankie.

I got up again. "I'd better take Callum home."

"I'll come with you," Rosie said. "I promised I wouldn't be late."

"Me too," Kenny said.

"And me." Lyndz gave the kitten a little pat. "Goodbye, kitten."

"What are you going to do with him?" I asked.

Frankie groaned. "I don't know. Maybe Mum'll have a brain transfer in the middle of the night. I'll think about it tomorrow."

We all went quiet. Poor Frankie.

There was a small scuffling noise behind the door.

"Ssssh!" Rosie held up her hand, and we all froze. Rosie tiptoed to the door – and flung it open.

Who do you think was there?

Unfortunately it was Callum, and he was grinning.

"It's the pest!" Frankie and Kenny wailed together, and Callum grinned even more.

"How long have you been there?" Rosie asked him.

"Shan't tell you," he said. "Are we going home now?"

"YES!" I said, and I marched him down the stairs.

On the way home Callum asked me again about rats.

"Kenny says she keeps hers in the garage," he said. "Do you think Mum would let me do that?"

"NO," I said.

"Maybe Dad would let me have a rat at his house," said Callum. "Maybe I could keep a rat in his garage."

"Callum," I said, "Frankie and Kenny are right. You're a PEST."

"No I'm not," Callum said, but he didn't sound as cross as he usually does when I call him that. "Can we go to the pet shop again after school tomorrow?"

"No," I said. "I've got things to do."

"*Please*!" Callum said. "If you do, I won't tell Mum you're going to spy on the lady who catches cats!"

"*What*?" I said.

Callum giggled. "I heard *lots* of what you said! You're going to be a spy! You're going to be a spy!" And he hopped up and down, singing in a silly voice.

"Actually," I said. "You heard wrong. It was *you* we were talking about... it's *you* that's the spy!"

"NO I'M NOT!" Callum shouted. "I'll tell Mum you said that!"

I sniffed. "Tell her what you like," I said. "*I'll* tell her *you* were listening outside Frankie's bedroom door!"

Callum shut up then. We walked the rest of the way home without saying anything.

CHAPTER SIX

When we met at school the next day Frankie was much more cheerful.

"I asked Mum about helping Mrs Brierley, and she said it was a mega-brilliant idea!" Frankie winked at Kenny. "She said it showed we were developing a sense of social responsibility, and she was really glad."

"Was she glad enough to let you keep the kitten?" Rosie asked.

Frankie frowned. "No. She said I had to take him back to the pet shop this afternoon."

"You can't," Kenny said. "It's half-day closing."

"Is it? Then I can keep him one more day!" Frankie brightened up at once. "He's getting ever so much tamer. He came down from the curtains almost as soon as I called him this morning!"

The horrible M&Ms went strolling past just then.

"Found your hot-water bottle yet?" they chorused, and then banged each other on the back with loud shrieks of laughter.

"They have to laugh at each other's jokes," Frankie said, very loudly. "No one else ever would."

"What's all that about a hot-water bottle?" It was Ryan Scott. I hadn't seen him coming, but he was suddenly right behind us. I started to smooth my hair down, but I stopped when I saw Frankie nudging Kenny. Frankie thinks I fancy Ryan Scott. Actually, I don't think there's anything wrong if I do. He's a very nice boy.

"Ryan – you don't want to know," Kenny said. "Those two are just *so* sad."

"They think it's funny to make jokes about my cat being lost," Lyndz told him. "She's been missing for three days now, and all they can do is make nerdish jokes."

Ryan looked really sympathetic. "My cat went missing once," he said.

"Did it come back?" I asked him.

"No," he said. "He'd been run over."

"Thanks a bunch," Lyndz said. "That makes me feel a whole lot better." And she went off across the playground. Frankie went with her, and so did Rosie and Kenny, but I didn't. I did think Ryan was trying to make Lyndz feel better, even if it didn't come out quite right.

"Tell you what," Ryan said, "tell Lyndsey she can come to my party. It's on Friday." I felt very strange right in the middle of my stomach. Ryan Scott was inviting *Lyndz* to his party! And not the rest of us! I think my mouth fell a bit open, because he gave me a funny look.

"I mean all of you," he said, as he spotted Danny McCloud. "Hey! Danny! Wait for me!" Then, as he dashed off to join Danny he shouted, "About seven o'clock! Bring any tapes you've got that are good!"

51

*   *   *

The others didn't think it was at all exciting that Ryan had asked us to his party.

"That's the night we're having a sleepover at my house," Lyndz said. "Don't you remember?"

"Couldn't we go the party and then have the sleepover afterwards?" I said. Frankie gave Kenny the sort of look that I know means they're sharing a joke and I'm not part of it.

"Who wants to go to Ryan Scott's party?" Kenny said. "It'll be full of boys with sweaty feet talking about football, football, football!"

"You like football," I said.

Frankie snorted. "We don't want to hear how Danny fell over in the mud seventeen times and Ryan would have scored if the goalie hadn't been in the way and how clever they all are."

"I wouldn't mind going," Rosie said. "We can talk about it afterwards! We don't need to stay for ages, but it might be fun for a little bit."

Lyndz said, "Why don't we vote?"

So we did, and Frankie and Kenny voted

against going. I was surprised when Lyndz voted yes with me and Rosie.

"I like the idea of talking about it afterwards," she explained. "And you never know – there might be someone at the party who's seen a missing cat!"

"We could make those notices about Truffle," I said. "You know – what she looks like, and your telephone number."

Lyndz gave me a huge smile. "Fliss," she said, "you may be wet when it comes to Ryan Scott, but you do have sensible ideas."

Even Frankie and Kenny thought it would be a good idea to go to the party after that.

I was very pleased, but when I started to talk about what we were going to wear they said to wait until Friday.

"Today is operation *spy* day!" Frankie said, and then the bell went and we had to go into school.

I was lucky. Callum goes out to tea with his weedy little friend Kevin on Wednesdays, so he wasn't hanging around when we reached

Frankie's house. Of course we had to rush in to say hello to the kitten. He was in Frankie's room, all curled up in a little fluffy ball inside a shoe box.

We all oohed and aahed. He looked utterly cute, but we didn't wake him up.

"Work first," Frankie said sternly, but I bet if he had been awake she would have been the first to cuddle him.

We went downstairs and down the road. I had butterflies in my stomach, and I think Rosie did as well. Mrs Brierley's house was quite big, and it had a high wall all round it. There was a gate, but it did look quite creepy.

"See?" Frankie whispered. "Once they're caught the cats can never get out again!"

"Yes they can," I said. "Lyndz saw one on the wall the other night."

"That's only after they've been totally brainwashed never ever to escape," Kenny said.

Lyndz made a face. "You can't brainwash cats," she said. "They do just what they want!"

"Who's going to knock?" I asked. I didn't

want to hear any more of Frankie and Kenny's stories.

Frankie looked at Kenny, and Kenny looked at Frankie.

"We had an idea!" Kenny said, and she began to giggle. "We thought that we should find out if Mrs Brierley really *is* a catnapper!"

"How?" I asked.

"Well," Frankie said, "if she *is*, she'll want to catch as many cats as she can, won't she?"

"I suppose so," I said. Rosie nodded.

"What do you mean?" Lyndz asked.

Frankie leant against the wall of Mrs Brierley's house. "Well – if she hears two poor lonely cats yowling in the road outside, she'll think 'Aha! Two more pussy cats for my collection!' And she'll come rushing out to get them!"

"But we haven't got two lonely cats," I said.

Kenny and Frankie began to giggle again. "Yes we have," Frankie said, and she began to meow... and then Kenny joined in!

"WOWWWLLLLL... MERRRRROWLLLLLL... WOWWLLL!!!!" they howled. "WOWWLLL!!!!!"

Lyndz, Rosie and I began to laugh too. They looked so funny, and they kept rolling their eyes as they howled.

CRASH!!! The window went up above our heads.

Frankie and Kenny stopped dead, but it was too late.

SPLASHHHH!!!!!! A bucket of water sploshed right over them – they were *soaked*!!!! And a little old voice called out, "Go away! Go away, you horrid cats!" And then the window slammed shut again.

I don't think I've ever laughed so much. My sides hurt, and so did my tummy. I ached all over. We leant against the wall in a row, and Frankie and Kenny dripped as they laughed.

"I think it's time for Plan B," Frankie said at last. "Well – after Kenny and I have zoomed home and changed."

"That's right," Kenny said. "Mrs Brierley certainly doesn't rush out to catch cats!" And she began to crack up all over again.

"What's Plan B?" I asked.

"We knock on the door," Frankie said.

"Mum's already told her we're coming."

"You mean she's expecting us?" I asked.

"Oh yes," Frankie said. "But we did just want to check it out first."

"Oh," Rosie said, and if she was feeling like me she was thinking Frankie might have told us that before.

Frankie and Kenny flew home to change. Kenny had to borrow some of Frankie's clothes, and they're really different shapes, so Kenny looked really odd! Frankie's tall and thin, and Kenny's much smaller. Frankie's jumper nearly came down to her knees!

"OK!" Frankie said. "Time for Plan B!"

CHAPTER SEVEN

It was a scary moment when Mrs Brierley opened the door. I mean, what if our experiment was wrong, and she really and truly *was* a catnapper? What could we do? And how would we know which cats were napped and which were properly hers? It suddenly seemed very difficult.

"Do come in," Mrs Brierley said, and it was the same little old lady voice we'd heard coming out of the window. She *was* little, too – she wasn't any taller than Lyndz.

"I do hope you won't mind," she said, "but I've got some tea ready for you. Just to say thank you." She sighed. "It's *so* nice to see some company. All I see from day to day is my sister, or my dear cats!"

We trundled into the kitchen.

ACE!!!!!

The table was positively groaning under the scrummiest, most mega-delicious, FANTASTIC tea you have EVER seen!

We stood and stared, out eyes popping out.

Mrs Brierley smiled and looked really happy. She had such a nice face we all smiled back, and I felt as if I'd been mean even *thinking* nasty things about her. I was glad I hadn't told stories about her having smelly fish heads in her bag and catching cats at night – even if it had been a joke. And I was very glad indeed I hadn't been howling outside her house… although I had laughed a lot.

The tea was the best ever. There was one cake with chocolate icing and one with coffee icing. There were buns, and biscuits, and scones, and jam, and a huge bowl of clotted cream. We sat down, and I don't think I've EVER eaten so much. It was going to be really difficult to bend to do any weeding!

Mrs Brierley liked seeing us eat. She kept offering us more and more, and she liked talking too. She told us the names of all her cats, and I felt worse and worse because she turned out to be the sort of person who would never, not in a million zillion years, collect a cat that didn't belong to her.

We talked a lot too. We told her about the Sleepover Club, and she thought it was a BRILLIANT idea.

"I wish I'd had such lovely friends when I was young," she said. "There are so many more things that children can do nowadays. Parties, and sleepovers, and pretty clothes."

"We're going to a party on Friday," I told her. "Before we have a sleepover at Lyndz's house."

"*Are* you?" Mrs Brierley twinkled all over her face. "And what are you going to wear?"

I was just beginning to tell her about my new skirt with little silver stars on and the matching top with silver ribbons when Rosie kicked me under the table. Kenny frowned at me over the chocolate cake.

"We're all going," Kenny said, "but we're only going because we want to see if anyone has seen Lyndz's cat. Ryan Scott isn't our favourite person. He needs to get a life beyond football!"

"I don't suppose *you've* seen Truffle?" Lyndz asked hopefully. "She's a dark brown tabby and she's got three white paws."

Mrs Brierley jumped up from the table, and her eyes were full of tears.

"Oh!" She said. "You poor dear thing! There's *nothing* worse than losing a cat, and not knowing where it could be, or if someone's being unkind to it! *Of course* I'll look out for it!" And she hurried round the table and stroked Lyndz's shoulder – just as if she was a cat! Lyndz looked surprised, but I think she liked it.

"And do any of you others have cats?" Mrs Brierley asked when she'd sat down again.

Frankie took a deep breath – and she told Mrs Brierley all about the little black kitten, and how it was exactly like Muffin. Mrs Brierley listened, and her eyes were so bright she looked like a little bird.

"Well," she said, "I think there's a very easy answer if you'd like it. Why don't you bring your kitten here? He'll still belong to you, and you can come and see him as often as you want. I can promise you he'll be happy – he'll have lots of other cats for company, and there's a big garden for him to play in!"

"Oh! That would be *lovely*!" Frankie jumped up, and she hugged Mrs Brierley. It was Mrs Brierley's turn to look surprised, but she beamed at Frankie. Her spectacles were crooked from the hug, but she didn't notice. "Just don't forget to ask your mother," she said. "I don't want you doing anything your parents don't know about."

"Can I get him now?" Frankie asked. "I mean – I'll ask Mum first – but if she says yes?"

Mrs Brierley nodded, and Frankie flew out of the door.

You'd have thought that the kitten had lived in Mrs Brierley's house all his life. Frankie carried him in squealing and squirming like a furry eel, but the moment she put him on the carpet he sat down, looked round and began to clean himself. He even began to purr like a tiny engine.

"Well!" Mrs Brierley said. "I can quite see why you fell in love with that one! Have you given him a name yet?"

Frankie sat down beside the kitten. "I thought I'd call him Muffin," she said. "Like my last cat."

"That's a fine name," Mrs Brierley said. "And it looks as if he feels at home! Now, would you like to see the garden?"

I think we'd all forgotten that that was why we were there! Mrs Brierley was so kind and nice that she wouldn't let us do much weeding, but if there are five of you it's far more fun than when you have to do it on your own. She had to tell us which were the weeds – Rosie had a big battle with something that looked like a huge thistle, and then Mrs B said it was a special kind and she was quite happy for it to go on growing.

(I did wonder if Mrs B was quite relieved

when we stopped gardening. She said we'd done a great job, but she looked a little bit anxious about the thistle thing.)

We went back to Frankie's house for five minutes before we all had to go home. Frankie didn't want to leave Muffin, but Mrs B said she could come over as often as she wanted, and any of the rest of us could come too.

"It'll do the cats good to see some new faces," she said. She also said she'd be sure to look out for Truffle.

"I do see stray cats round here sometimes," she said. "In fact, there were a couple of horrible old tom cats fighting outside in the road earlier. I don't think they'll be howling outside my house again, though. I was very hardhearted and taught them a little lesson."

We couldn't say anything when Mrs B said that about the tom cats. Rosie made a gulping noise, and Kenny gave a sort of cough. Then we thanked her very very much indeed, and off we went.

On the way back we make a vow. We held hands and promised that we'd *always* look after Mrs Brierley.

"Do you think we should tell her that *we* are the tom cats?" Kenny asked.

Lyndz began to laugh. "I think she knew!"

"WHAT?" Rosie, Frankie, Kenny and I stared at her.

"Didn't you notice?" Lyndz said. "She never asked you two why your hair was wet. That was *weird*! I mean, how often do girls come to visit wearing odd clothes with drippy hair?"

"Oh." Kenny looked thoughtful. "And she did say she'd taught them a lesson—"

"She certainly did!" Rosie said. "You should have seen your faces when the water came down!" And we began to laugh all over again.

CHAPTER EIGHT

I had another good idea the next morning. Yes, I know that's boasting, but my mum always says that if you don't tell people when you're clever how can they ever know?

I was on my way to school and Callum was going ON and ON and ON about rats when I had my idea. Why didn't we ask Mrs Weaver if we could write and print out the notice about Truffle at school? The school computers are ace – you can do different borders and typefaces and rainbow colours.

I met Rosie and Kenny first, and they thought it was a dead smart idea, so we tried it out on Mrs Weaver when we saw her walking across the playground.

"Sounds like a good idea to me," she said. "Maybe we could get the whole class involved – a piece of descriptive writing that will wring the heart of anyone who reads it!" And she went into the staffroom.

Frankie and Lyndz arrived next, and they were keen too, although they weren't sure about the whole class having a go.

"We only need to use the ones we like," Kenny pointed out. "And we can run off lots of copies of those so we have plenty to take to Ryan's party."

"We don't want to be giving leaflets out *all* the time," I said.

Kenny tweaked my hair. "It's OK, Miss Flutter Heart. I'm sure there'll be loads of time for you to make eyes at Ryan and dazzle him with your starry skirt."

"How did you know I had a starry skirt?" I said.

"Don't you remember?" Frankie did a twirl under my nose. "You were giving Mrs B a stitch by stitch description for hours and hours yesterday."

"No I wasn't!" I said. "Kenny kicked me and I stopped!"

"I *didn't*!" Kenny said. "It was an accident!"

"OOOOOH!" It was the M&Ms. "Arguing, are we? And we thought you lot all cuddled up together with your hot water bottles!"

They staggered off holding each other up.

Rosie made a face. "Isn't it time you thought of a new joke?" she shouted after them.

"They're the saddest thing on earth," Frankie said in disgust.

"We're really going to have to do something about the M&Ms," Kenny agreed. "Anybody got any good ideas?"

But we hadn't.

When Mrs Weaver told everyone that we were all going to write a description of a cat and then think of a short piece of writing to go with it the only people who groaned were – guess!

YES!!! The M&Ms.

Mrs Weaver fixed them with a steely gaze. "Emma and Emily," she said, "I shall be particularly interested to see what you write. You are both clever girls, so I'm sure you will think of something suitable."

The M&Ms sat up and looked smug. "Can we work together, Miss?" they asked.

"That will be fine," Mrs Weaver said.

We all got into pairs or threes, but before we started to write Mrs Weaver asked Lyndz to stand up and describe Truffle. Then Mrs Weaver said were there any questions? Danny said something silly about did Truffle live in a chocolate box, but no one else asked anything. We all settled down to write.

After a while Mrs Weaver asked if any of us had finished, and would we like to read out what we'd written?

Lyndz went first. She read:

"Truffle is a special cat because I love her so much. She isn't very pretty, except I think she is. She is a dark brown tabby with three white paws, and is quite fluffy. When she left home she was wearing a green collar. The collar has my telephone number on it. If you have seen her PLEASE phone me – because I miss her."

Mrs Weaver said that was excellent, and then she went over to the M&Ms' table.

"Now, Emma and Emily," she said, "what have *you* done?"

They both smirked. It's the only word I can think of that exactly describes the look on their faces. Then Emma read out:

"Truffle is a pussy cat
Who warms my toes at night.
Her coat is brown and tabby
With three paws fluffy white.
Please tell me if you see her,
Skipping out there in the street,
And if you do please tell me,
Because she's very, very sweet."

Everybody clapped except us. Kenny and Lyndz looked at each other, and I saw Kenny cross her eyes. Frankie made being-sick noises, but very quietly, and Rosie rolled her eyes at me.

Of course Mrs Weaver thought the poem was stunningly clever and ace and the most excellent ever written.

"There, Lyndsey!" she said. "Wouldn't you like to use Emma and Emily's poem? I'm sure they wouldn't mind. I'll set the computer up for you at lunchtime… and I think you should thank them for their hard work."

Lyndz squirmed about in her seat, and then muttered, "Thanks a lot." The M&Ms sat and smirked and smirked.

Frankie stood up. "Please, Mrs Weaver, I think Lyndz should use her own piece of writing!"

Mrs Weaver didn't look that impressed. "Frankie," she said, "it was you and Lyndsey that suggested it should be a class project. I don't think you can change your minds now – especially when Emma and Emily have written such a lovely poem."

Frankie sat down.

*   *   *

The rest of the morning was one of the most gruesome we've ever lived through. The M&Ms never stopped grinning like a pair of horrible gargoyles, and they offered to write poems for everybody in the class. Even Mrs Weaver got fed up in the end, and told them to be quiet.

At lunchtime we stayed in and printed about twenty copies of the M&Ms' pathetic poem, and Mrs Weaver gave us a box to put them in to keep them clean. We left the box on the table by the computer; we didn't feel like taking it home.

"You don't have to use those," Rosie said as we trailed out.

"No," Frankie said. "We could type out your one on Dad's computer tonight."

Lyndz groaned. "Fancy having to *thank* the M&Ms. And I can't come round tonight. Mum says it's time I came straight home after school for once."

"Me too," Rosie said. "Are we still going to Ryan's party tomorrow? And then having a sleepover?"

"I'm not even sure about that," Lyndz said gloomily. "Mum was saying something about some old school friend of hers coming for the weekend. I'll tell you tomorrow."

The bell went, and we drooped back into afternoon school. It didn't feel as if anything was going to go right for us EVER again... but then things changed!

CHAPTER NINE

It was after school. We were chatting while I waited for Callum, when Rosie suddenly realised she'd left her bag behind. She dashed back into the classroom, and – *there were the M&Ms, secretly printing out loads of copies of their poem!!!*

As you can imagine, Rosie came zooming back to tell us.

"When they saw me," Rosie said breathlessly, "they switched the screen off double quick, but I could see the pile – even though Emma was trying to sit on it."

Our mouths fell open so wide they nearly

hit the concrete floor.

I just stared.

"Why ever would they do that?" Kenny asked.

"What did they say?" said Frankie.

"What did *you* say?" said Lyndz

Rosie grinned a wicked grin. "I remembered about being a detective," she said. "I waved, grabbed my bag and ran. I banged the door behind me as I went out... and then I crouched down outside and listened!"

"COOL!" said Frankie. "What did you hear?"

"I couldn't hear what they were saying," Rosie said. "But I heard the printer running again as soon as I was outside the door – so I *know* they think I didn't see anything."

"WOW!" Kenny's eyes were shining. "Those M&Ms are up to something again – but this time I think we might be one step ahead!"

"So what should we do?" I asked.

"One of us ought to sneak back in," Lyndz said. "See what they're doing now."

"I can't," Rosie said. "They'll be suspicious if it's me."

"HEY!" Kenny gave a huge jump in the air. "I've got it! Fliss, *you* can go! You can ask them if they've seen Callum!"

"ACE!!!" Frankie banged Kenny on the back. "They'll never suspect Fliss! They'll just think the pest has escaped again!"

I was halfway back to the classroom when I met the M&Ms coming towards me.

"Hi!" I said, "have you seen Callum?"

"Dear me," Emily said, "have you lost him? How careless! First it's a cat, then a brother! Mind you count your fingers and toes tonight!"

I didn't answer. I walked straight past.

Of course I knew Callum wouldn't be in the classroom – but I still went in. I thought I might do a little detecting too. The computer was switched off and everything was tidy – until I saw the wastepaper bin. It was stuffed full of crumpled up sheets of paper.

CLUES!!!! I thought, and I grabbed the top couple of sheets.

It was their poem, just as Rosie had thought. The two copies I had were a bit blurry, so they must have thrown them out. I stood up, and glanced at it – and then I froze. I really did! You read about people freezing in stories, but I've never known what it meant before. But it's true – your arms and legs feel totally switched off. But my brain was working. I could still read. And this is what I read:

"Truffle is a pussy cat
Who warms my toes at night.
Her coat is brown and tabby
With three paws fluffy white.
Please tell me if you see her,
Skipping out there in the street,
And when you do please tell her,
I promise to wash my smelly feet!"

I wanted to zoom back to the others yelling at the top of my voice, but I didn't. I looked at all the other sheets of paper in the bin. The M&Ms had been working on the poem and changing bits, but – and isn't this a mega-brilliant bit of detective work? – I detected that the sheets on the top must have been the last dropped in the bin – so *that* must have been what they'd been printing out when Rosie saw them! I stuffed the two sheets of paper in my pockets and hared right out of school.

Kenny and Lyndz were sitting on the bench when I came bursting out. Rosie and Kenny were talking to Callum, who was looking very grumpy. What's new?

"I want to go HOME!!!" he said as soon as he saw me. "I want to go NOW!!!"

"Callum," I said, "if you are *very, very* good and give me *ten* minutes we'll go home past the pet shop."

That shut him up. He went skipping off to the water fountain.

The Sleepover Gang could tell from my face that I'd found something!!!! I reached into my pocket, and snatched out the pieces of paper with a flourish. Rosie grabbed one and Kenny grabbed the other, and Frankie and Lyndz peered over their shoulders.

"This is just that awful poem," Frankie said.

"What's so special about— OH!"

Lyndz and Kenny got to the same bit at the same time.

"RIGHT!!!" Kenny yelled. "This is WAR!!!"

They read it again. And again.

"Well done, Fliss," Lyndz said, and I glowed.

"What are we going to do now?" I asked.

Frankie was screwing up her face. "You know what I think? I think the M&Ms are going to swap the poems – so when we get to Ryan's party everybody reads *this* load of garbage!!!"

We stared at her. It seemed obvious now she had said it.

"Was our box of poems still there?" Frankie asked me.

"Yes," I said. "It was on the table."

"I know!" Kenny said. "Why don't we take our poems out of the box, and put something HORRIBLE in it instead – something that'll really make them shriek?"

"SPIDERS!" Rosie said. "We could fill it full of spiders!"

"YUCK!!!!!" I said. "I'm not catching spiders – not even to scare the M&Ms!"

"Nor me," Lyndz said.

"I can catch spiders," said a squeaky voice just behind us.

We jumped – it was Callum.

I was about to shriek at him for listening in to our conversation *again* when Kenny stopped me.

"Can you really catch spiders, Callum?" she asked.

"'Course I can," he said. "How many do you want? There's LOADS and LOADS in our shed."

"No there aren't!" I said.

Callum looked rather pink. "Yes, there *are*. I put them there."

Rosie clamped her hand over my mouth. "Well done, Callum!" she said. "Can you bring them to school tomorrow?"

Callum nodded. "Can I have them back after?"

"NO!!!!" I said.

"Callum," Kenny said, "if you bring the spiders in you can come to my house and play with my rat. Promise. Cross my heart and hope to die."

Callum thought about it. Then he looked at me. "And can we still go to the pet shop on the way home? You did say."

I gave in. "Yes," I said.

"FAB!!" Frankie began to dance around the playground. "Hey – Fliss – make sure you get here before the bell! And we'll have to watch those two *extra* carefully to make sure they don't swap the poems before we've done our dirty deed!!!!!"

"Help!" Rosie looked at her watch. "I've got to go! Mum'll *kill* me!"

"Me too," Lyndz said.

"Can we go now?" Callum said.

"Yes," I said, and we did.

The next morning Callum and I walked to school one behind the other. Oh, I know the spiders were in a box inside another box, but I wasn't taking any chances.

The others were waiting.

"COOL!" Kenny said. "When will we put them in the box?"

"We'll have to do it at break time," Rosie said.

"I'll put the box on our table until then so they won't be able to fiddle with it."

"Do you know," Lyndz said slowly, "I think they'll try at the end of the day… in case we notice."

"That's settled, then," Frankie said. "Oh – and don't forget to bring your pyjamas tomorrow night. Mum says it's OK if we have a sleepover after the party."

"BRILLIANT!!!"

The morning dragged until break time. I kept looking at Kenny's bag. I knew the box of spiders was inside – what if they got out? But at least they had two boxes to eat their way through. YUCKKKK!!!!

Then – would you believe it? – when break time finally came it was raining, so it was wet play and nobody went out of the classroom at all. The only thing that cheered us up was that the M&Ms kept winking at each other, and sniggering. They had something planned – that was for sure. And they asked us about three times each if we were going to the party, and if we were going to give everyone one of their poems. Rosie had a secret peep to see if they'd already done a swap, but they hadn't.

It had stopped raining by lunchtime.

"Mrs Weaver, shall we tidy up the classroom?" Emily asked in her sweetest be-nice-to-the-teacher voice. "Emma doesn't feel very well, so we'd rather not go out."

We held our breath.

"No, Emily," Mrs Weaver said firmly. "You've been in all morning – a blast of fresh air will do you both good." And she swept us all out in a no-nonsense sort of way.

"Oh – Mrs Weaver!" Frankie popped up beside her. "Can I fetch my jumper from the coat pegs?"

"Hurry up, then," Mrs Weaver said, and Frankie scooted off, with a wink to us.

I don't think we've ever hurried back after lunch before – but this time we did. It was OK – we were there before the M&Ms. Mrs Weaver had stopped them in the corridor to ask

Emma how she was feeling – they looked *so* fed up!

I was even more nervous in the afternoon. The box was back on the table by the computer – but now I knew it was full of spiders! But first we had maths, and then we had history – and then – I can hardly tell you for laughing!

It was very nearly the end of school. We were all twitching. What if we'd been wrong? What if the M&Ms *weren't* planning to swap their poem for ours? And then Emily got up, and went over to the computer.

"Mrs Weaver," she said, "can I type out my project?"

Mrs Weaver was busy, so she just nodded. Emma got up next, and went over to the computer too… carrying her bag. She bent down, winked at Emily and pulled a pile of papers out of her bag – and then knocked our box on to the floor.

SCREAM!!!!!! The M&Ms were standing on the computer table clutching each other and shrieking their heads off. Paper was scattered all round them, while half a dozen fat spiders were heading for dark corners as fast as they could go.

OK, I admit it. I screamed too. *And* I leapt on to our table.

Mrs Weaver was *so* angry. She actually shouted at us all to be quiet ... and *then* she picked up one of the pieces of paper. She only glanced at it at first, but then she frowned.

"What EXACTLY is going on here?" she asked.

And then it all came out. The M&Ms were so shaken that they told Mrs Weaver exactly what they'd done...

PHEW!!!!! We *almost* felt sorry for the M&Ms. But of course, there were the spiders to explain. So – we got a major earwigging too. We're all picking litter off the playground every break next week. But it was worth it!!!!

CHAPTER TEN

I bet you thought that was the end! But it isn't – because I haven't told you about the party.

No, it's OK. I know you may not want to know about what I wore – though it did look very nice. (No, I'm *not* boasting. Ryan said so. And so did Lyndz.) No – I wanted to tell you the most AMAZING thing.

We'd arranged to meet outside so we could all go in together. We always do that at parties. It means you don't have to stand around on your own. Anyway, Lyndz was the last to arrive. She looked puffed out.

"What's up?" Kenny said.

"Dad took me round to the cats' home," Lyndz said. "After all that fuss with the M&Ms I suddenly thought we *still* haven't done anything about finding poor Truffle. Dad was feeling sympathetic, so we went to look – but she wasn't there." Lyndz gave a huge sigh. "I think she's gone forever." And a tear rolled down her cheek.

Then Frankie did one of the nicest things ever. She swallowed hard, and she said, "Lyndz – if you like, you can have Muffin. He'll make you feel better – really, he will."

Lyndz shook her head. "Thanks, Frankie," she said. "But I don't want another cat. Not yet. I want Truffle. But thank you."

Frankie gave a sort of cough. "Let's go and get this over with," she said, and she rang Ryan's door bell.

Ryan's mum opened the door – and there, *right in the middle of the hall,* was Truffle!!!! She was was looking very thin, and her front paw was bandaged – but we all knew it was her. She knew Lyndz, too. She began to purr the loudest purr you ever heard – and Lyndz sat down on the doorstep and cuddled her and hugged her.

Ryan's mum was very nice. She told us she'd found Truffle crying in her back garden with her paw swollen right up. She'd taken her to the vet, and he'd treated the paw, but no one knew where Truffle came from. She wasn't wearing her collar – so it must have fallen off somewhere.

"Didn't Ryan tell you we'd taken in a lost cat?" she asked.

"No," Frankie said, and she looked very hard at Ryan when he came out to see what all the noise was.

Ryan went as pink as Callum does when he's done something wrong. "I didn't think it was your cat, honestly," he said. "You said yours had a green collar. And—" he shuffled his feet, "it was really nice having a cat again."

His mum gave him a funny look – half cross, half not. "But you can't have this one, Ryan," she said. "Not if it belongs to Lyndsey." She looked thoughtful for a minute while Ryan looked at the ground. "But how about we go to Mr Garez's pet shop tomorrow and see if he has any kittens for sale?"

Ryan looked so pleased I thought he was going to burst. "Really?" he said and when his mum nodded he squeezed her *so* hard. Then he saw us all looking and coughed and tried to look cool. But we knew he was thrilled really.

So – it was all happy endings. Lyndz had Truffle back, and when we had our sleepover that night Truffle sat on her toes *all* night, and Lyndz wouldn't move so we had to pass her biscuits and coke and stuff as if she was a queen or something.

And there are *more* happy endings! Muffin is EVER so happy at Mrs Brierley's house, and is growing huger and huger every day. We're always popping round to see him, *and* Mrs B of course.

What else? Oh – you remember Frankie's mum saying she couldn't have a kitten because of something that was going to happen next summer? Some kind of surprise? Did you guess what it was? I didn't.

FRANKIE'S MUM IS HAVING A BABY!!!!!

Frankie is so thrilled – you'd think no one had ever had a baby before. She's quite nice to Callum when he comes round to see Kenny's rat – I think she's practising on him.

One last thing. Don't laugh. Promise? Ryan asked me to go with him to collect his kitten.

This is Felicity Diana Sidebotham saying, "Thank you very much for your company."

See you!

Sleepover Girls go Designer

Rosie is really miserable — her dad has gone off on holiday instead of decorating her bedroom as promised. The Sleepover Club decide to do-it-themselves instead. All the materials are bought and ready to use... what could possibly go wrong?

Unfortunately, quite a lot does go wrong, and sleepovers for the foreseeable future are banned! Is this finally the end of the Sleepover Club...?

Pack up your sleepover kit and drop in on the fun!

0 00 67422-8

The Sleepover Club Surfs the Net

Frankie is hooked up to the Internet on her home computer and Rosie finds a competition to design a Home Page, with fab prizes for the winners and runners-up.

The Home Page has to be for a club that the entrants belong to. It takes clever Frankie to point out that they do all belong to a club — the Sleepover Club! After much cutting and sticking and staying up late, the girls' entry is ready for posting, but will it reach the competition organisers on time?

Pack up your sleepover kit and drop in on the fun!

0 00 675445-7

Anastasia Krupnik

Anastasia opened her green notebook and,
in a secret corner, very small, she wrote the
most terrible name she could think of. She
closed the notebook, and smiled.

Anastasia Krupnik is ten, and two very
important things are happening to her: A
small pink wart appears on her left thumb:
and she discovers that she'll soon be having
a quite unnecessary baby brother.

Serious action is called for, but the only
reason she hasn't left home yet is that she
has been allowed to choose the baby's
name...